Maisy's Garden
Sticker Book

Lucy Cousins

Take the sticker pages out of the middle of this book.
Open the pages so the stickers and the pictures
in the book can be seen side by side.
Read the words on each page.
Then choose which sticker to peel off
and where to put it in each picture.

CANDLEWICK PRESS
CAMBRIDGE, MASSACHUSETTS

Maisy is in her garden.

Maisy and Tallulah paint the shed.

Dress them
in their
painting
smocks.

Find Cyril's wheelbarrow.

It's time for
a picnic!
There are good
things to eat
and drink.

A day in the garden is lots of fun! Bye-bye, Maisy.